CAT PROBLEMS

by Jory John
illustrated by Lane Smith

RANDOM HOUSE STUDIO ▲ NEW YORK

To William, Olive, Ferris Mewler, Kurt, and Zoe.
—J.J.

To A.J., Noodle, Pretzel, Wizzy, and Lulu.
—L.S.

Text copyright © 2021 by Jory John
Jacket art and interior illustrations copyright © 2021 by Lane Smith
All rights reserved. Published in the United States by Random House Studio,
an imprint of Random House Children's Books, a division of Penguin Random House LLC, New York.
Random House Studio and the colophon are registered trademarks of Penguin Random House LLC.
Visit us on the Web! rhcbooks.com
Educators and librarians, for a variety of teaching tools, visit us at RHTeachersLibrarians.com
Library of Congress Cataloging-in-Publication Data is available upon request.
ISBN 978-0-593-30213-2 (trade) — ISBN 978-0-593-30214-9 (lib. bdg.) — ISBN 978-0-593-30215-6 (ebook)
The illustrations for this book were created in oil paint mixed with cold wax and digitally in Procreate.
MANUFACTURED IN CHINA
10 9 8 7 6 5 4
First Edition

Book design by Molly Leach

Where's that sunbeam going?

HEY!

SUNBEAM!
GET BACK HERE!

Great.

Now I'm wide awake,
and I only got nineteen
hours of sleep.

Sigh.

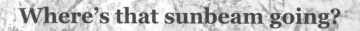

Ahem.

You're in my spot.

That's where I curl up,
sometimes.

Now you're in my
other spot.

Now you're in my **_third_** spot.

I think that cat might
be my greatest enemy
in the entire house.

My paws are dirty.

Blech.

I guess it's time for my
seventeenth bath of the week.

A little privacy, *please.*

Hey, look,

an empty box.

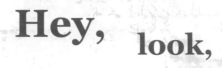

Now what?

My eyelids are getting heavy . . .

. . . heavier . . .

. . . *heaviest* . . .

THUMP!

VROOOOOOOM!

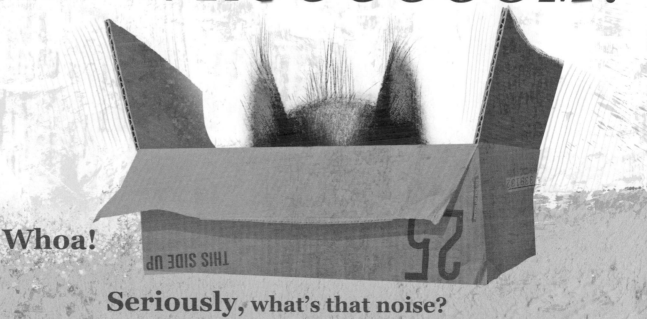

Whoa!

Seriously, what's that noise?

Now what?

Hmm.

I guess I'll bat this piece of foil around.

bat bat bat

Sigh . . .

What's the point?

I gotta get out
of this house.

I think that monster's gone.

For now.

I need to know what's going
on in every room of this place.

I want to eat
that plant.

I want
to chomp
that book.

I want to scratch the couch, but I already tore all the material off both arms.

I want to rip that curtain.

But hey, that's just me.

You're in my spot. Again.

You're in my *other* spot.

Why am I even *standing* here?

Like, this is pretty random, even for *me*.

Things would be
different if I knew
how to open a door.

I haven't been outside in eight years.

Sigh.

I'm trapped in this *house* all the time.

I just go from room to room with nothing to *do*!

You! Cat! Hello!

I confess that I have watched you mope

Now listen to me, Cat: Somebody feeds you.

Somebody gives you water.

you warm and even hands you treats.

around outside, hiding nuts that I'll never again locate,

Things are difficult out here, Cat.

This tree, although it's shared with roommates.

which I'm saving for some reason. A button.

Sure, you may be housebound, and you may

current living situation, but look at *me*, Kitty.

O U T S I D E ? Honestly, what I

a *touch* of boredom from time to time. **Yes,**

paw to trade places with you for a day.

And start embracing the life you have.

will fall into place after that.

Think about

I spy you through this window.

around your house for *months*.

Somebody changes your litter box.

Somebody brushes you and keeps

Treats, I say! Meanwhile, I scurry

evading predators that only seem to multiply.

I don't have much. My branch, of course.

A few nuts I've kept. A piece of ribbon,

A n d   t h a t ' s   a b o u t   i t .

find reasons to gripe about your

You think it's so great

wouldn't give for just

I would give my right

So quit saying, "Poor me."

Everything else

it . . .

How can I eat this very
talkative squirrel?

Hmm.

He's lucky there's this
window screen separating us.

Things would
be different if
I knew how to open
window screens.

I have nothing to do, and I'm vaguely hungry.

Maybe I'll meow for a while.

Let's see how this plays out . . .

Mraowww! Mraowww! Mraowww!
Mraowww! Mraowww! Mraowww!
Mraowww! Mraowww! Mraowww!
Mraowww! Mraowww! Mraowww!
Mraowww! Mraowww! Mraowww!
Mraowww! Mraowww! Mraowww!
Mraowww! Mraowww! Mraowww!
Mraowww! Mraowww! Mraowww!
Mraowww! Mraowww! Mraowww!
Mraowww! Mraowww! Mraowww!

Let's try this again . . .

Mraowww! Mraowww! Mraowww!
Mraowww! Mraowww! Mraowww!
Mraowww! Mraowww! Mraowww!
Mraowww! Mraowww! Mraowww!
Mraowww! Mraowww! Mraowww!
Mraowww! Mraowww! Mraowww!
Mraowww! Mraowww! Mraowww!
Mraowww! Mraowww! Mraowww!
Mraowww! Mraowww! Mraowww!
Mraowww! Mraowww! Mraowww!
Mraowww! Mraowww! Mraowww!
Mraowww! Mraowww! Mraowww!
Mraowww! Mraowww! Mraowww!
Mraowww! Mraowww! Mraowww!
Mraowww! Mraowww! Mraowww!
Mraowww! Mraowww! Mraowww!

Yesssss!
My whole day has led me to this wet food.
This is a highlight, for sure.
And that says quite a lot about my day.

I guess it's okay in here.

Sometimes.

munch, munch, munch

Yum.
That's not bad.
Not bad at all.

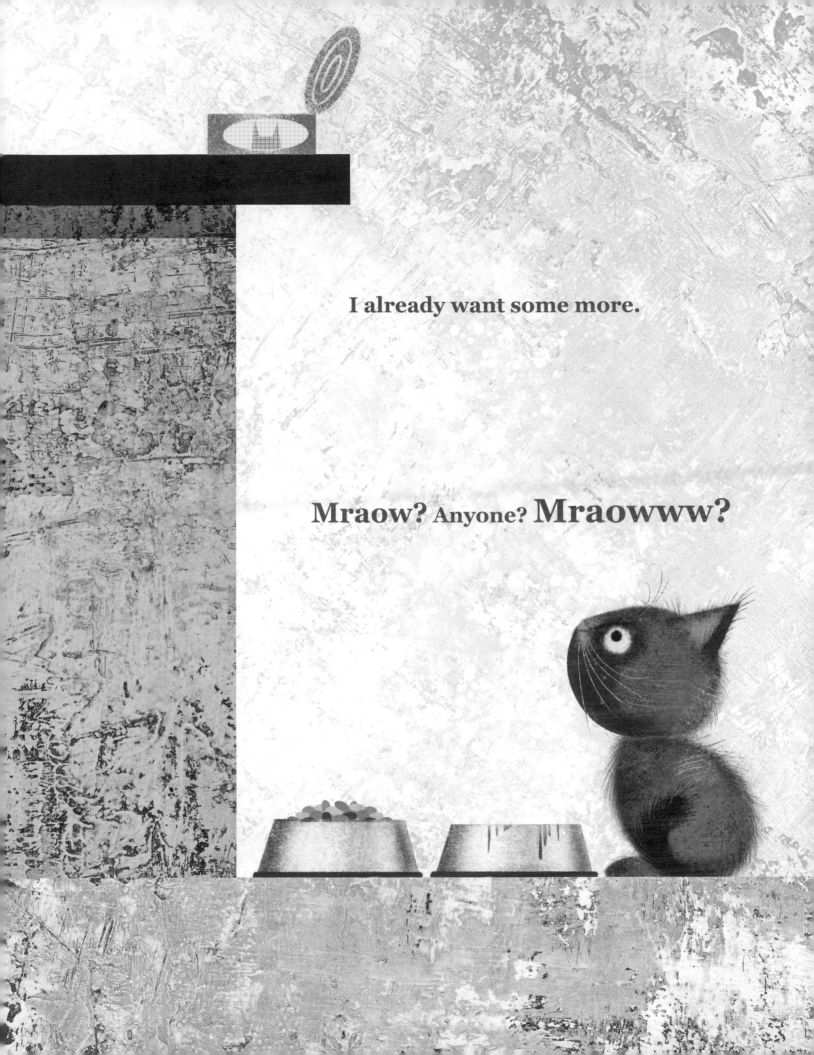

I already want some more.

Mraow? Anyone? **Mraowww?**

Hmm.

Now what?

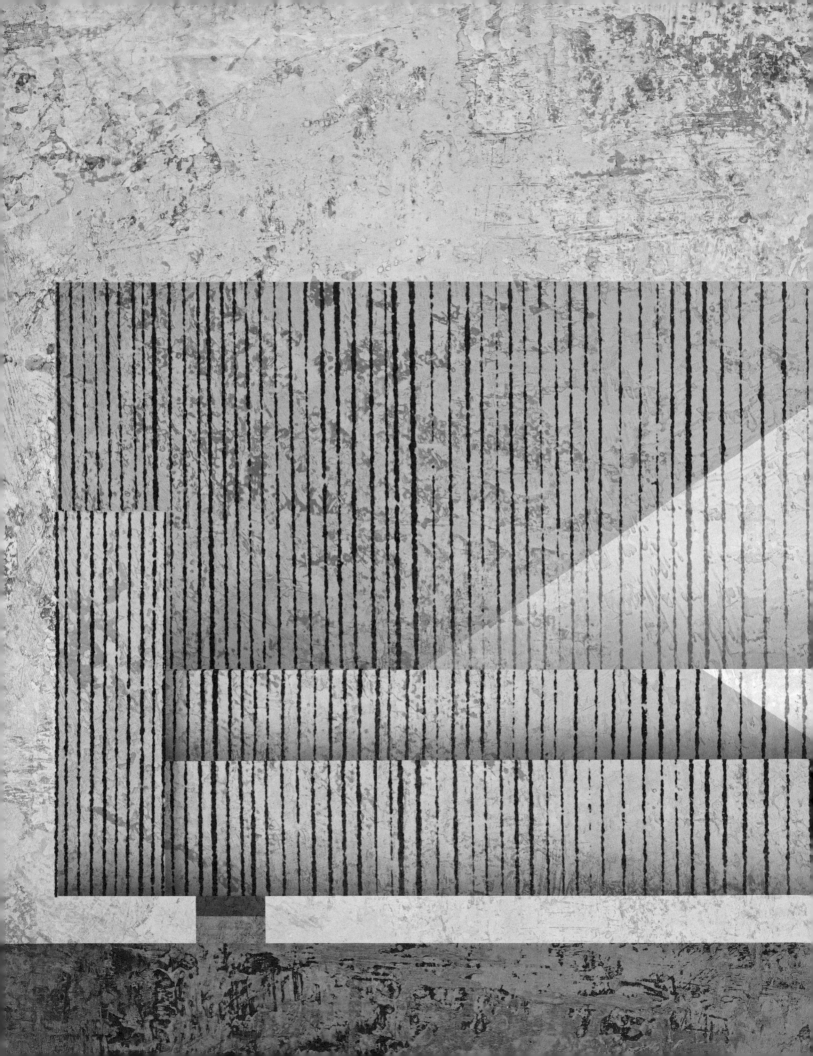

You're in my spot.

When's that sunbeam coming back?